D1107621

NO LONGER PROPERTY OF
THE SEATTLE PUBLIC LIBRARY

To all insomniacs, for one reason or another. —M. C.

Text and illustrations copyright © 2023 by Marianna Coppo.
All rights reserved. No part of this book may be reproduced in any form
without written permission from the publisher.

Library of Congress Cataloging-in-Publication Data available.

ISBN 978-1-7972-0443-7

Manufactured in China.

Design by Lydia Ortiz.
English translation by Debbie Bibo.
Typeset in Brandon Grotesque.
The illustrations in this book were rendered in tempera and pastels.

10 9 8 7 6 5 4 3 2 1

Chronicle Books LLC
680 Second Street
San Francisco, California 94107

Chronicle Books—we see things differently.
Become part of our community at www.chroniclekids.com.

FiSH AND CRAB

Marianna Coppo

NO LONGER PROPERTY OF
THE SEATTLE PUBLIC LIBRARY

chronicle books · san francisco

It's nighttime again.

All is quiet in the aquarium.

Good night,
Snail.

Good night,
Starfish.

Good night,
Oyster.

Good night,
Fish and Crab.

It's time to sleep.

Ah. Finally!

click

Crab?

Are you sleeping?

Umph. YES.

Oh, okay. Sorry!

I can't sleep, either.
I'm a little worried.

Uh-huh.
Now please stop talking,
and try to sleep.

Oh, okay.

CRAB!

Did you hear
that noise?

**Yes,
it's your voice.**

No, no.
I mean that
ooh, ooh.

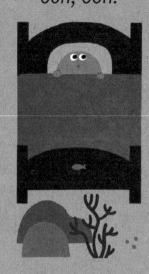

**There is no
*ooh, ooh.***

Well, there was
BEFORE.

Sure.

**Anyway,
it's gone now,
so go to sleep!**

Okay, but . . . what if
it was an owl?
Do owls eat fish?

There are no owls here.
And, anyway, NO—I don't
think owls eat fish.
PLEASE STOP.

Maybe it was a mouse?

**We are in an aquarium!
There are no mice in aquariums.
No mice, no owls, and no lions,
in case you were wondering.**

Oh dear,
I really hope not!

But what about . . .

OH BOY.
This cannot go on.

I'm going to make
you some herbal tea.

And then I want you to tell me
ALL your worries.
ALL OF THEM, all at once.
And when you're done, we will both
finally go to sleep.

Oh wow—thanks, Crab!
Now, where was I?
Oh yes, I remember.
What if . . .

aliens abduct us while we're sleeping
and we wake up on another planet?

What if we sleep too much
and wake up in the distant future?

Is it a future I can sleep in?

What if it
rains frogs?

FISH
AND
CRAB

What if a black hole
opens and sucks us in

and we end up in
a parallel universe

where I am you and you are me?

Now THAT is really scary.
I mean, the part about you being
me and me being you.

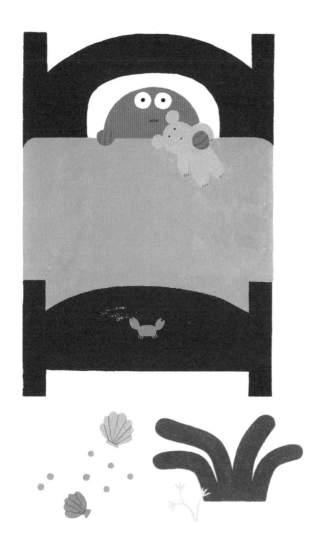

What if I get chicken pox
and don't notice because I'm red?
I could be contagious.

WHAT IF WE ARE CHARACTERS IN A BOOK?

Well, that's it.
I feel much better now.
Thank you, Crab.
Good night!

Fish . . . ?